Alila

Our Little Philippine Cousin

Mary Hazelton Blanchard Wade

Edition : Culturea (Hérault, 34)
Contact : infos@culturea.fr
Print in Germany by Books on Demand
Design and layout : Derek Murphy
Layout : Reedsy (https://reedsy.com/)
ISBN : 9791041818686
Légal deposit : July 2023

ALILA Our Little Philippine Cousin

CHAPTER I
THE NEW BABY

Alila is such a strong, active boy now, it is hard to imagine him in his babyhood,—he was such a tiny brown tot!

His nose was so flat one would hardly have noticed there was a nose at all, except for the wideness of the nostrils. His big black eyes seemed to be moving around all the time, as much as to say:

"I must find out everything I can, and just as fast as I can, about this queer place in which I find myself."

His hair was straight and coarse and black, even on the day he was born. It was quite warm (in fact, almost all the days are warm in the Philippines), yet the doorway was carefully covered and the windows closed tightly.

Now, why do you suppose Alila found himself shut up in a close room like that when he first entered this big round world of ours, while there was such a soft gentle breeze outside as scarcely to move the tops of the cacao-trees in the garden?

The fact is, Alila's father, who is not afraid of the wild buffalo nor the boa-constrictor, nor even the huge cayman, is constantly dreading the evil that bad spirits may bring to him. And now he had a darling boy of his very own! According to the beliefs of his people, no evil spirit must be allowed to enter a home when a child is born, or the little one might be troubled by the spirit for the rest of his life.

So the loving parent walked back and forth over the roof waving a bolo in his hand, as much as to say:
"Look out, spirits, or you may get your throats cut. Keep away from here. Do not try to get inside to trouble my little one."

He did this very earnestly in the first hour of Alila's life, although he was shown the foolishness of such ideas by the priests the Spaniards sent among his people.

He is a small man, this father of Alila. He has high cheek-bones like the Chinese and Japanese, and no beard upon his face.

When he felt that everything was really safe, he climbed down from the thatched roof, and, opening the door as little as possible, went softly up to the mat where the baby lay and kissed him.

But, dear me! not all persons kiss the way we do, and this father of the Malay race seemed rather to smell the baby than anything else we can think of. He placed his own nose and lips on the baby's cheek and drew a long breath. It was done to show his love, and that is what any kiss is given for, is it not?

This baby's bed would not, perhaps, suit all the other babies in the world. Some of those babies we know are cared for on cushions of down and wrapped in soft flannels and delicate muslins. But what did black-eyed Alila care for that? To be sure, he lay on a mat of woven palm leaves, but it was sweet and fresh.

And although the floor his eyes sometimes rested on was not covered with a rich velvet carpet, it was smooth and clean, for it was made of split bamboos flattened and fitted close together. And oh, that floor was beautifully polished by Mother Nature herself, for the bamboos as they grow are covered on the outside with a coating of the finest and hardest varnish.

If Alila could have thought about it at all, he would have considered himself more fortunate than most babies,—for did not his own dear mother, who lay at his side, make every bit of the spread which covered his tiny body? She had taken the fibres of pineapple leaves and hemp and woven them together.

But that alone would not make the spread beautiful enough for her dear one. It must be given a bright colour, so she searched through the woods till she found a sapan-wood tree; then, breaking off some branches and opening them, she took a substance from the heart of each and made a crimson dye.

So you can see that the cover was done entirely by Alila's mother; and you can ask yourself if that wasn't a hundred times better than buying cloth out of a store. That would not have the touch of love in its making.

There was something else in Alila's home one does not see in other lands. Whenever the baby's eyes turned toward the light, they found it very soft and restful, for it came through a window in which were fitted the inner shells of a certain kind of oyster.

It was so pretty! The colours of the rainbow shone there in pale tints, and the flaring sunshine could not enter. The room was kept in a sort of twilight all day long, and made it pleasant for the new-born baby and his mamma to doze and dream.

CHAPTER II
HIS FIRST PARTY

Alila was not two hours old before friends began to arrive to see him. But they did not enter suddenly! That would have been the height of rudeness. As they reached the doorway, each in turn stood for a long time on the outside, making many complimentary remarks to Alila's family. That was their way of showing themselves well-mannered and polite.

The Tagals, for that is the name of this tribe of people, never do anything suddenly. They do not appear to believe in surprise parties.

When all the fine speeches which seemed proper had been made, they entered the little house and came to the side of the new baby. They made the young mother very proud by the praise they gave her tiny son.

But she and her husband were not the only ones pleased. There was Alila's grandmother, who was always the most honoured one in the household; there was also an aunt who made her home here as she was too poor to have one of her own; and beside these, there was a lame old man, a friend of the family, who had come to them for shelter. The Tagals are so hospitable they will never turn any one from their homes.

As one visitor after another arrived, the little house became crowded. If it had not been for the high, dome-shaped roof, the air would have grown heavy and impure. As it was, Alila and his mother soon grew very tired and closed their eyes in sleep.

"That is good," said the grandmother, "we must let her rest. We will go out under the cacao-trees and talk, and I will bring some cocoa wine and betel to you there."

This old woman was certainly not pretty, although good and thoughtful. As she stood talking to the visitors in low tones, one could see how short she was. Her coarse, black hair grew down upon her forehead almost to her eyebrows; her wrinkled skin was dark brown; her eyes were large and round and, like her baby grandchild's, ever turning in a new direction.

She was dressed in a short skirt much like those of the other women of the party; it was of three colours,—green, white, and bright red. Over this she wore a large piece of blue cotton cloth, cut in the shape of an oblong, tucked in at the waist and hanging over her skirt almost down to her knees. No shoes or stockings covered the bare legs or feet, but she did not seem to miss them.

She was as straight as an arrow, even if she were a grandmother. Perhaps it was because she had been used to carrying jars of water and baskets of fruit upon her head ever since she was a little child.

She moved softly about the hut as she got the entertainment ready for the company. From one corner she drew forth a large bamboo with a grass stopple in it. This held the wine the guests would sip so sparingly, for the Tagals are a sober people and seldom drink enough fermented liquor to hurt them. The old woman next got some cocoanut shells together. These were the only drinking-cups the family ever used.

But the betel which she now placed beside the other things,—what is that, you ask? It is not a food, and yet it often takes the place of food; for a Tagal can work a long time without eating if he can chew all of this he wishes. It is prepared from the nut of the areca palm, one of the most beautiful trees in the world. A palm of this kind grows right beside Alila's home, and, now that he is a big boy, he climbs the tall tree himself and brings down the nuts which grow at the top under the tuft of glossy green leaves.

The nuts are cut into thin slices and wrapped in the leaves of a singular plant called buyo. But, before they can be used for this purpose, these leaves are coated with lime made from oyster shells and then folded up.

Alila's grandmother prepared a quantity of betel before the new baby was born.

Just as she was going out to offer refreshments, another visitor arrived. It was a friend who had come from a distance, but the mother and child must not be wakened. Oh, no! that was not to be thought of. The souls of people leave their bodies and go away while they are sleeping, the old woman believes; and if any one should arouse them suddenly, they might never return to their bodies.

So, of course, the visitor, who also had this belief, wouldn't have disturbed the sleepers for anything in the world. She quietly turned away and joined the other guests in the garden.

CHAPTER III
THE CHRISTENING

Alila was christened soon after he was born. Dear me, what a time that was! The festival lasted several days. There was a host of friends and acquaintances around the little home, making merry and admiring the baby.

Mother holding baby up in the air
"HIS MOTHER HAD BATHED HIM IN THE WATER OF THE RIVER"
Alila himself was as clean and sweet as any child in the world could be. His mother had bathed him in the water of the river which flowed down the mountainside near them, while the leaves of the papaw-tree took the place of soap.

The young mother herself was only fifteen years old. She was dressed in her brightest skirt and fairly shone with the abundance of cheap jewelry she wore. Her hair was combed straight back from her forehead. She wore nothing on her feet excepting her queer slippers, of which she seemed very proud. She had herself embroidered them to look like a pair worn by the rich lady whose husband owned the plantation. They were perfectly flat and had only uppers enough to encase two or three toes.

What queer, uncomfortable things to wear on one's feet! Alila will never own such things because he is a boy, and he should be glad of it.

His grandmother and aunt had a fine feast prepared for the visitors. There was a good supply of roasted buffalo and wild boar's meat. There was a salad made from the young green tops of the bamboo; steamed rice and stewed iguana; papaws, which tasted like melons; tamarind sauce and guavas and bananas. And, of course, there was an abundance of betel, cocoa wine and tuba.

But strangest of all the dishes at the Tagal's feast was one prepared from a kind of beetle. The guests relished it greatly and Alila's father was praised very much for surprising them with this dainty.

But the feast was only a small part of the entertainment. A band came from the village to furnish music. Every instrument on which they played was made of bamboo. Then there was dancing and singing under the palm-trees by old and young, and when evening came there were displays of fireworks.

As Alila's father was quite poor, how could he afford such splendour? The fact is, it cost him nothing! It was a free show given by Mother Nature. Her little children, the fireflies, gathered in great numbers and danced in circles around the trees. Any one ought to be satisfied with fireworks like those.

Alila's eyes watched the people eat with their fingers and looked at the lights dancing about; he listened to the odd, sweet music for a little while; and then those black eyes closed tightly and he lay fast asleep in his young mother's arms. Of course, he doesn't remember anything about it now, but his grandmother has told him the story so many times it almost seems as though his own mind had kept the pictures for him.

CHAPTER IV
THE BUILDING OF THE HOUSE

And now he is a big boy, ten years old, and can do so many things to help his parents. He has not always lived in the home where he was born. Last summer a whirlwind destroyed that one, but he helped his father build another just like the first, and he showed himself a very clever worker.

He searched through the forest for bamboos of the right size; he did his share in cutting them down and splitting them for the walls of the hut. When they were ready, he worked each morning in thatching the roof until it grew too warm. Then came dinner and a nap under the trees until the late afternoon, when work began again.

In a few days a new home was ready and the terrible hurricane forgotten by the carefree, happy little boy.

Can you guess what part of the hut took the largest share of Alila's time and attention? It must have been the window-panes, for he was anxious to get the most beautiful mother-of-pearl he could find. He had to take a trip to the seashore ten miles away, and then he spent many hours finding such oyster shells as had a very delicate lining.

"The two windows must be beauties," said the boy to himself, "for that will please my mother so much."

No carpenter's shop nor store was visited during the whole time. It was not needful, for the forest near by stretched its arms toward the workers, as much as to say: "Come to me; I will gladly give you everything you can possibly wish."

"How about nails," you ask, "and stout cord with which to fasten all the parts together?"

Nails, and a bolt in the door? Why, what could be better than a stick of rattan, cut and whittled into shape? Cord? That was obtained very easily, too, from a bushrope-tree growing near Alila's home. It is so stout and strong it is not an easy thing to break it.

When the house was finished, it looked like a great beehive. There was only one room, but what of that? If people are perfectly comfortable they can be as happy in a one-roomed hut as though they lived in a palace.

Alila has so many good times you would almost envy him. In the first place, it takes him only a minute to dress in the morning. A pair of thin trousers and a shirt hanging down outside instead of being tucked in at the waist, and his toilet is made.

When he goes out into the sunlight, he wears an odd-looking hat of rattan. It is made in the shape of a cone, and shields his eyes nicely from the sunshine. He goes to no school, so he does not know how to write to his new American brothers, but that doesn't trouble him in the least.

He always has enough to eat, and is satisfied with a dinner of rice and fish any day. Besides, there is always a bunch of bananas hanging inside the house, and he has sugar-cane in abundance.

He is hardly ever punished and is allowed to do very much as he pleases. It is fortunate that he pleases to do right nearly all the time.

He swims every day in the river; he fishes from his bamboo raft; he hunts in the forest with his father. His chief duty on the sugar plantation is to keep the monkeys out of the cane. It was not long ago that he shot two of the mischievous little fellows with his bow and arrow and hung the poor things on poles like scarecrows to frighten others away.

CHAPTER V
FOUR-FOOTED FRIENDS

Alila has a tame monkey at home now. He has taught him many clever tricks. Every night when he goes to bed, the monkey curls himself up by his side and lies there till morning. He seems to love his little master very dearly and often rides on his shoulder while Alila is working.

Until a few months ago, the boy has lived on a sugar plantation owned by a rich Tagal planter. The plantation is divided up into small farms and rented to different workmen. The planter furnishes one buffalo and all the needed tools to care for each little place.

When the harvest time arrives in December, each tenant carries his crop to the mill for grinding. He is allowed one-third of it for himself, and, whatever price it brings, it must support his family for the next year.

boy riding pull

"SOMETIMES ALILA RIDES ON HIS BACK"

Alila is not the least afraid of his father's buffalo. When he was only three years old the huge creature would obey him and allow him to drive anywhere he pleased. He seemed to know by the tone of the boy's voice just what he wished him to do.

It made an odd picture,—the tiny little fellow, holding a slender rein in his chubby hands as he trotted along by the buffalo's side. The rein was fastened to a piece of split rattan drawn through the animal's nose. Yet somehow every motion of Alila was understood by him. Is it the boy's patience that makes the beast so gentle? We like to think so.

If we should take Alila's place the animal would not stir to obey us. He would at once become stubborn and ugly, because he is not used to our quick, nervous, impatient ways.

He cannot work all day like a horse. After two or three hours, he needs to stop and rest. But that is not enough,—he suffers if he cannot have a bath. Sometimes Alila rides on his back when he plunges into the river, and holds on without fear while the buffalo stretches his head down and holds it under the water for two minutes at a time as he searches for food.

How Alila does love him! He has the next place in his heart to his father and mother. But the buffalo has other good friends beside Alila's family. They are not people, nor even other buffaloes. They are white herons that follow him as he ploughs. They are not afraid if Alila is the only person there. As the animal's heavy feet plod over the ground, worms and insects come to the surface. The herons know this and easily get a good breakfast.

Besides these attendants, a small blackbird often keeps the buffalo company, who will raise up his head in delight to meet it. Why is it? Because the bird flies about his head and neck and picks off the insects from his skin.

This buffalo has lived on the farm from the time he was caught wild when a baby. If he had not been so young he could never have been tamed. A wild buffalo is a terrible thing; he is most to be dreaded of any creature in the islands.

CHAPTER VI
THE BUFFALO HUNT

Alila's father has been on several buffalo hunts, but never yet has he allowed his boy to go with him. He says it is far too dangerous; the little boy must wait until he is older. But it is so hard to wait, Alila thinks, as he longs for the time to come and looks up at the pair of horns brought home from the last hunt.

The horns are very long and curved and sharp. The boy often wonders if there is another animal in the world with such fearful horns. He says to himself:

"Perhaps the very buffalo who owned this pair was the one that gored to death poor Olo." Alila stretched himself on the ground, closed his eyes, and again pictured the story in his mind. This is the tale:

In the village just below the plantation there lived a young man who was honest and brave but very poor. It happened that he loved the daughter of a neighbour very dearly and she returned his love. But the youth had no money and no land, and at first the girl's father said:

"No, you cannot have my daughter, for you can give her no wedding portion."

It is the custom among these people for the lover to give his bride as fine a present as her parents think suitable. The young man felt very sad, when an idea entered his mind that gave him hope. He said to the father:

"Can I not come to your farm and serve you for two years? And if I then show myself faithful in all my duties, will you give me your daughter?"

The father consented. It was a very common thing for such service to be given, and he felt satisfied.

The two years passed by. The young man had worked day after day at the hardest labour. He had never spoken a cross word nor found the slightest fault. But now that his service was over and the day set for his marriage, he wished to show the father of the lovely girl how brave he was, and he wanted to make his bride some little present, too.

He heard that a party of men, one of whom was Alila's father, were going on a buffalo hunt. He would join them. It was to be his first venture of this kind, but he had no fear.

The party was made up of six men on horseback, two tame buffaloes, and a pack of immense dogs used to hunting. The men were armed with knives and spears and each one carried a lasso.

They started in the early morning and rode out over the plains till they came to the edge of a large forest. There they waited at some little distance from an opening through the trees while the dogs were sent into the forest to rouse the prey. They had only a short time to wait before the barking of the dogs was heard.

They took their places some distance from each other and listened breathless. The young lover was to be given the first chance in this combat. A bull-fight is fearful enough, but it cannot compare with the struggle between a maddened buffalo and his pursuer.

Hark! There is a crashing of trees, a falling of branches. The ground shakes and out from the darkness of the forest plunges a huge buffalo. He raises a storm of dust as he comes onward. He is shining black, and as he tosses his head one can see the wicked horns, capable of doing such terrible injury.

For an instant he pauses and looks at the men standing ready to capture him; then he rushes toward the young man, who now has the chance he begged for. With lasso in hand he urges his horse toward the buffalo.

It is over in a moment's time. He has hurled his lasso but has failed; and before he can move out of danger the furious animal has thrown him from his horse and ended his life.

But the other hunters cannot stop a second. They, too, will lose their lives if they are not careful and quick. One after another gallops after the enraged animal and throws his lasso. There are several failures, but each time the men manage to escape. At last two are successful, and the monster, hardly able to breathe, stands quiet and still.

He is conquered. And now other lassos are drawn tightly around that magnificent head and the animal is tied to the stout trunk of a tree. The danger is over for these others, but the poor youth who longed so greatly to succeed lies dead not far away. He will never see his dear one again.

The men lift his body tenderly and carry it to the place where the tame buffaloes have been left. They place it on the back of one of them. Then they return to their prey and fasten a rattan ring through his nose. With one of the tame buffaloes on each side of him, he can now be easily led to the village, where they will kill him.

All the people came out to meet the hunters, and, when they heard the sad news, all hearts were filled with pity for the young bride.

CHAPTER VII
THE RICH MAN'S HOME

One day as the boy lay dreaming of the time when he should be allowed to risk his life in a buffalo hunt, his quick ear heard the steps of some one coming down the road. He jumped up and saw an old friend of his father's, a well-known hunter. He carried a basket in each hand and would not have stopped if Alila had not called out:

"Where have you been the last few days? And where are you going? Father will be home soon and he will wish to see you."

"I am on my way to the master's house to sell these bird's nests and I will stop here on my way back. I expect a good price for them. He told me he would pay me well. Ah, but it was hard work getting them, my little fellow! You never could have done it in the world."

Alila looked at the hunter with envy, for he knew how dangerous his work had been. Among many people in the East, no food is thought so great a dainty as these edible birds' nests. What queer tastes they have! At least it seems so to us.

There is a certain kind of bird that makes its nest high up on the sides of steep cliffs jutting out over the waters of the ocean. These nests are like no others. The birds that build them swallow a certain kind of glutinous weed growing on the coral rocks. They then cough it up and use this material they have so oddly prepared in making their nests.

Whenever a man makes it his business to search for these nests, he knows the danger full well. Slowly and painfully he must climb the sides of the cliffs, often placing his feet where we should think there was no foothold whatever. He clutches at a sharp point of rock here, or a twig there; but if it is not as safe as he believed, woe unto him! For down he falls into the raging waters below and is a lucky man if he is not dashed to pieces on the sharp rocks. Again, he may grow faint and dizzy when he has climbed only a part of the way, or he may lose his hold from very weakness.

The Chinese are as fond of these edible birds' nests as are the Filipinos. Perhaps you have heard of the great Chinese viceroy, Li Hung Chang, who came to visit us several years ago. He brought his own cooks and a large supply of birds' nests and sharks' fins.

Alila joined the hunter on his way to the planter's mansion. The boy wished to have a chance to see the grand lady, the planter's wife, and their little daughter, who plays so beautifully on the harp.

They soon reached the house, which seemed very large beside Alila's little cabin. It was two stories high. The lower part was of stone and the upper half of wood. It would not have been safe to use stone above the lower floor on account of the frequent earthquakes.

The roof was thatched with cogon grass. When it was built the planter said to himself: "I will not have an iron roof like many of the city houses; it would be too hot. I like the grass thatching much better."

Beautiful gardens where roses were always in bloom surrounded the house. Bright-coloured birds flew about among the bushes, but they had no songs for Alila and the hunter as they passed along. The broad veranda was shaded by a clump of tall banana-trees, swaying to and fro in the gentle breeze. How noble they looked, with their tufts of glossy leaves at the very top, lapping over each other and shutting out the sun's hot rays!

As Alila glanced up to see if the fruit was ripening the hunter said:

"Did you ever hear the stories told of the banana? Some say it is the very fruit that tempted Eve in the Garden of Eden, while others think that she and Adam made their first clothing of banana leaves."

"I wonder if that can be so," said the little boy, thoughtfully. "Any way, I'm glad there is fresh fruit every month in the year; I like bananas so much."

They reached the house as he finished speaking. The planter and his wife were sitting alone on the veranda. Alila was disappointed in not seeing their little daughter.

While the hunter was attending to his business with the planter, the boy's bright eyes noted the lady's dress.

"I must tell mother all about it," he said to himself. "She will want to know. My, what a long train she wears! It is so thin and delicate I think it must be woven of pineapple fibre. What beautiful bright colours it has!

"And how stiff her kerchief is! It stands up so high at the back of her neck I should think it would feel very uncomfortable. Her chemisette is very pretty, my mother would think. What wide sleeves! Still they are short, so she can keep cool."

But the jewels! Alila had never seen so many before. The lady fairly sparkled, with her gold earrings and bracelets, set with precious stones. Surely there was going to be a party at the big house, or she would not be dressed so finely.

Just as the boy was thinking this, the planter's wife turned her head toward him and spoke.

"Alila, is it not time to tap the cocoanut-trees? Tell your father I want some tuba as soon as possible. You are now such a big boy, I suppose you will be able to help him get it."

The little fellow made a low bow and answered that his father had spoken about it that very morning and had promised that he should help him. Perhaps you remember that when Alila was christened there was a good supply of tuba at the feast. Did you wonder what it could be?

On the sugar farm there is a clump of cocoanut-trees on which no fruit ever grows. Why is this? Because all the sap which would be used by Mother Nature in making blossoms and changing these into cocoanuts is used for another purpose. It is drawn from the tree at a certain time of the year to make a drink much loved by the natives.

Tapping the trees for tuba is dangerous work, but Alila, you know, loves danger. He went home from the planter's mansion very happy, for now he should have an errand there every day during the next few weeks. For must he not bring the family a fresh bamboo of tuba each night and morning?

CHAPTER VIII
TAPPING FOR TUBA

Alila was wide awake before sunrise of the next day. He did not lie on his mat lazily watching to see if a lizard or newt should creep out of a corner, as he often did on other mornings. It was only the day before that he pulled a newt by its tail just to see if the tail would really come off in his hand. It did, for a fact! and away Mr. Newt scuttled without any tail.

Wasn't it a little cruel and ungrateful in Alila, when he knew how much the newts as well as the lizards do to let him sleep comfortably? They destroy ants and spiders and other creeping things, so that Alila's mother never kills them nor drives them away.

Neither did Alila stop to play with his pet cat this morning—such an odd cat, too, with a queer little twist in her tail like that of a pug dog. Alila was dressed before his father waked.

While waiting, he went out into the yard to sharpen his knife. But he had no whetstone. There are more ways than one of doing things, we have already discovered. The boy took a piece of wood and covered it with a paste made of ashes and oil. Then he rubbed the blade of his knife back and forth over this till the edge was sharp enough to split a hair with ease.

Next he got together some vessels of bamboo and two long bamboo rods. He was just a little bit nervous, although it was not in his nature to be easily excited. He said to himself:

"Oh, dear, I hope I shall not have to wait much longer."

At this very moment he looked up and there was his kind, quiet father standing in the doorway.

Boy climbing palm tree
"HE WAS AS NIMBLE AS A SQUIRREL"
"All ready!" And the two started for the cocoanut grove not far away.

As soon as they reached the place, Alila took out his sharp knife. Work began at once, for notches must be cut in the tree, one above another, in which to place his toes. As one notch was made, the boy drew himself high enough to get a foothold in it; then, reaching up, he cut the next one and drew himself up to that, and so on until he had reached the top, fully sixty feet above the ground. A cocoanut-tree, as you probably remember, has no branches whatever to give any help to a person in climbing.

And now Alila came down again. He did it so easily and gracefully, it was a pleasure to watch him. As soon as he was within reach, his father handed him vessels of bamboo, which the boy fastened to his waist and again climbed the tree. One might almost say he was as nimble as a squirrel, yet that does not express the long, graceful movements of his body as he rose far from the ground.

When he was once more at the top of the tree, he made deep cuts in the trunk directly under the great tuft of leaves, and hung his bamboo vessels so the sap could flow into them.

Now for the same work in the next tree. Do you think he must go down to the ground again and go through all the work he had in climbing the first tree? Not at all. His father reached up to him two long bamboo rods. He took the first one and stretched it across to the next tree. This would serve as a bridge over which he could walk. The second one was placed above the first and would make a good hand-rail.

Alila did not think of the danger of a walk in mid-air on such a slender support. His head was cool, his feet were firm, his body light, and he passed from one tree to another in perfect safety. He was happy as a king to be trusted by his father to take such a risk.

Think of a fall from a height like that! Suppose for one instant that the bamboo should give way under the boy's feet or failed to hold in the tree-top! That would have ended our little Alila's life in a moment, or at least made him a cripple for the rest of his days.

The fact is, however, that the boy had no accident, and every day afterward, as long as the sap continued to flow, he went out to the cocoanut grove, collected the tuba, and carried a good supply of it to the planter's mansion.

CHAPTER IX
FOREST AND STREAM

There is another cocoanut grove on the farm, beside the one where Alila gets the tuba. The fruit is allowed to ripen on these trees, and it is the boy's duty to gather it. There is a new growth of cocoanuts three times a year.

Alila does not need to climb the trees for them unless he wishes. He usually fastens a sickle-shaped knife to the end of a long pole. In this way he can reach up to the tops of the tallest trees and cut off the cocoanuts; when thud! thud! down they fall to the ground, safe and sound. For the delicious pulp is not only shut up in the hard shell that we know, but this also is enclosed in a still larger and thicker covering.

How could the natives of tropic lands get along without this valuable tree? It has so many uses it would take a long time even to mention them all.

Its roots are good to cure Alila when he is seized by an attack of fever during the wet season. His mother believes that his life has been spared through the use of this medicine. Alila's father made his canoe from the trunk of a cocoanut-tree; while much of the furniture in his employer's mansion has been carved from its beautiful wood. The boy's mother uses a comb made from the stalks of cocoanut leaves. The husks which enclose the fruit are made into coir, out of which are made ropes, brooms, brushes, and even bedding.

When Alila was only five or six years old he learned to weave baskets and mats from the leaves, and he knows how to thatch a roof with them very neatly.

What is so delicious on a hot day as a drink of fresh cocoanut milk! It is never hurtful and quenches the thirst as well as the coldest water. The oil obtained from the nuts is used by Alila's mother in her cooking.

But she also needs it for another purpose. She is always in fear of an earthquake, and feels safer to have a light burning in readiness all night long. She keeps in the cabin a small vessel half-full of water. Cocoanut oil is poured on the water and a wick made of a certain kind of pith called tinsin hangs down in the middle of this odd lamp. The Chinese taught the Tagals the value of tinsin. There is scarcely to be found a native hut where it is not used for lamp wicks.

But you must be tired of hearing about cocoanuts and their uses, so we will return to Alila and his strange adventures. One day not long ago his mother said to him:

"My child, I should like some fish for dinner. Will you go to the river and get some?"

Alila has great success in fishing. He started off at once on his errand. He did not stop to get hook and line, as you would have done; he knew another way to fish, different from any we have in our country.

When he got to the river he walked along by its side till he found a place where the water ran very deep. Then he took off his clothing, and lay quietly down on the bank. His eyes were wide open and watchful, though his body was so still. He soon saw some fish rise near the surface of the water. Quick as a flash he jumped in and dived down, down under where the fish were darting. Rising as suddenly as he had dived, he came to the surface with a fish in each hand.

He is such a nimble little fellow that he did this several times, and hardly ever failed. It was not long before he had a fine string of fish to carry home. As he walked back, he stopped to gather some green bamboos of medium size, for he knew they would be needed in cooking the dinner.

While his mother was cleaning the fish, Alila made a fire and cut the bamboos at every joint. They were changed at once into baking pans, each one large enough to slip a fish inside, together with a little water and some spices. The ends were stopped up, and the bamboos laid in the fire. As soon as they began to burn, it was a sign that the fish inside were cooked enough.

What a good dinner it was! You would have thought so if you could have tasted the rice steamed in the same way as the delicate fish and served on plantain leaves.

Alila has still another way of fishing which is not as hard work as diving, though, after all, it is not much fun. He carries a bamboo basket in which he has put a mixture containing a curious kind of poison. He sets it floating on the water. When the fish come near it the poison makes them stupid, and they rise and float motionless on the surface, as though they were dead. Then it is an easy matter for Alila to get them.

CHAPTER X
A SWARM OF LOCUSTS

The little brown boy has lived, as you know, on a sugar plantation, where the cane ripens only once a year. You also remember that last summer a hurricane destroyed the boy's home, and a new one had to be built. The sugar crop barely escaped ruin, when, alas! another danger came to it, more fearful even than the great wind. It was a storm of locusts.

Alila was working in the cane-fields with his loved buffalo one morning, when, looking up suddenly, he saw something which frightened him. It was a long distance away, far as his eyes could see, and it appeared like a dark cloud near the earth.

people trying to wave off swam of locusts
"SUCH A DIN AND COMMOTION YOU NEVER HEARD"
The boy was frightened, as I have said, but it was not for himself. It was on account of the danger threatening the plantation; he knew very well that what seemed like a cloud was composed of millions and millions of locusts. Unless something were done at once, all the sugar-cane would be ruined. For, if that army of insects, perfectly harmless to animals, should settle down upon the canes, the leaves would be entirely eaten in a few hours.

Alila ran as fast as his legs could carry him from one part of the plantation to another, and gave the alarm to the working people as he passed along.

It was wonderful how quickly men, women, and children armed themselves to meet the coming enemy. All the bamboo clappers, cocoanut shells, tin pans, and red flags that could be found were seized and put into use.

Then such a din and commotion you never heard nor saw, even on the glorious Fourth of July. Locusts are very sensitive to noise, so between the beating of drums and clappers, the waving of the red flags, and the smoke from fires of wet wood at the sides of the fields, the greater part of the army passed on. The people breathed again, since the danger was over for the present.

When it was all over Alila was not too tired to play for awhile with a few locusts he had caught in a net. Their bodies looked like those of large grasshoppers, except that they were of a brownish colour.

They would not sting or bite, and the boy kept his new pets as long as they lived. That was only a few days, however, as a locust has a very short life. It is said that food passes through its body as fast as it is eaten, so it is not nourished, and soon dies for this reason. It also has an enemy, a small worm that forms in its body and gradually eats it up.

The mother locust has a queer way of making a nest for her eggs. She extends the end of her body till it is like an auger, and with this she bores a deep hole in the earth. She chooses spots near fields of ripening rice or sugar cane, so the young locusts, as they hatch out, will be near a good supply of food; for at first they have no wings and cannot go in search of it.

After the visit of the locusts, Alila went carefully around the edges of the fields with the other workmen. They wished to see if any signs of young locusts could be found. But they found none and felt that the crops were free from danger for this year, at least. But Alila's father said to himself:

"How many risks there are in working on a sugar plantation! I have been here now many years. I never know whether the crop will be a failure or not. I believe I will go somewhere else. Up on the side of the mountain, not far from here, is a large hemp plantation; I will seek work there. Besides, there is fine hunting near by and Alila can see new sights."

When he told his family, they were all pleased, for Tagals dearly love a change and often move from place to place merely for the sake of change. Alila was the most delighted of all. He said:

"Now, father, I can hunt with you and go bat shooting in the deep forests. You know I can sell their beautiful soft skins to travellers."

Alila's grandmother and mother were pleased, too. They liked the idea because the hemp is gathered throughout the year and can be sold from time to time, whenever there is need of money. But when the women thought of the bands of brigands who hide in the mountain passes, they began to fear.

Many were the stories they had heard of these robbers and their sudden attacks in the night-time on people in lonely houses.

"You need not worry," said Alila's father, "for these wild robbers seldom harm poor people; and they never kill unless they are obliged to do so. I believe they are not as terrible as they are often described."

CHAPTER XI
THE NEW HOME

So it came to pass that Alila went to a new home. It was not hard work to get ready, for there was little to move. The old buffalo that had grown up with his young master was able to carry on his broad back everything owned by the entire family. He could easily have taken more, too!

The women rode on ponies and the men walked beside the buffalo. No one seemed to feel sad, although it had been an easy, happy life on the little farm and the sugar planter had always been kind.

Their fellow workmen were Tagals like themselves; they would find many Chinese labourers on the hemp plantation, at least they had been told so. But they did not care for that.

There are many Chinamen in the Philippines, and they agree very well with their Tagal neighbours and the people of the many other tribes. Alila has a cousin married to a Chinese merchant in Manila and some time he is going to visit her.

As they journeyed onward they passed a party of Americans. Alila's mother called:

"Come nearer to me, my child. Stay by my side."

She had a fear of white faces of which she could not rid herself. The Spaniards had been cruel to her people, she well knew. And now that these others from far-away lands had taken the power from the Spaniards, she felt that they, too, would be hard and unkind.

Poor ignorant mother! She did not understand that it meant such different things,—schools for all children instead of a very few; work for any one who desired it; better care for the sick in the cities; fewer taxes for all. Yes, all these and many other good things would be done by the Americans to make Alila and Alila's children live more wisely and therefore more happily.

When the sun was setting that night, the hemp plantation could be plainly seen. It was a beautiful sight, those rows of small trees with their large, glossy leaves, shut in by woods of a larger growth.

The plant from which is made what is called Manila hemp belongs to the same family as the banana and the plantain. The leaves all of them look so much alike it would be hard for us to tell the difference.

It did not take many days to get settled. The neighbours were very kind and gave the family shelter and food until Alila and his father had finished building a cabin. This time they made the roof as well as the sides of the hut of split bamboo, and the boy's mother and grandmother helped in preparing it.

Alila had never before seen hemp gathered, and he had much to learn. He was soon very quick in separating the fibres from the pulp and spreading them out to dry before packing.

The boy sometimes wonders what journeys the bales of hemp will take. To what countries will they sail? To what uses will they be put? His father has told him that nothing else in his island home is shipped in such quantities as Manila hemp. It makes stout cordage and sail-cloth; it is woven into mats, carpets, and hammocks; while the finest hemp is made into delicate dress goods for the rich ladies of the island.

Yes, people all over the world have heard of Manila hemp, and when he is older, Alila says he will bear it company and seek strange sights across the oceans.

He had lived in his new home but a short time when he had an exciting adventure. Not far from the farm there is a dense forest. One night Alila's father said to his friends:

"Let us go on a hunt for wild boars. There must be plenty of boars and deer, too, in those woods."

The other men were ready for a little sport. They had been hunting in the forest many times before, and knew the best course to take.

"May I go with you, too?" whispered Alila, who was listening at his father's side.

When all agreed that it would make no trouble to allow the boy to go with them, since he was brave and strong, he was greatly pleased. They would be gone several days. What new, strange creatures should he see? What dangers should he meet?

CHAPTER XII
IN THE FOREST

The party started out early the next morning. They carried very little food with them; it would only be in their way when hunting, and they trusted Mother Nature would supply what they needed as they went along. Two of the men had guns; the others carried bows and arrows. Every one was also supplied with a sharp spear and knife.

The first day was very quiet. Nothing was shot but a few birds and bats. When night came they found themselves far from any stream; all were thirsty and there was no water. What should they do? Ah! in plain sight was a liana. It is called the "travellers' drink" because any one, on breaking off a stalk, can obtain a cool draught. How refreshing it was!

A fire was quickly made and the birds cooked for supper. They all lay down to sleep. But, alas! that was not an easy thing to get. They had no sooner stretched themselves by the fire than they were attacked. By wild animals, you think at once. By no means. It was a small enemy, fierce for their blood, which darted out from the grass and fastened upon their bodies.

Multitudes of leeches have their home in the mountain forests of the Philippines, and every native who travels there is armed with a small rattan knife to cut them off as they seize upon him.

Alila's party knew that sleep was out of the question for this night. As fast as our little brown brother was able to cut off one of the bloodthirsty creatures, another took its place, till at last the daylight came and the hunters could go on their way.

But what a wretched sight they were! Blood streamed from their arms and legs, and they looked like the wounded survivors of a terrible battle. When they came to a spring of water, they were glad enough to have a chance to bathe.

Alila can tell you that was the worst night he ever passed in his life, yet he hardly spoke a word of complaint through the long hours, and in the morning laughed gaily with his friends when they gazed at each other's sorry-looking faces.

Small creatures can make themselves as troublesome as big ones. Perhaps you have already found this out when mosquitoes have found their way to your bedside and waked you in the middle of the night.

After a hasty breakfast, the hunters were ready for a tramp, and they soon found the tracks of wild boars. It was not long till they had killed three of them with little trouble. They were about to make a fire and roast some of the flesh for dinner, when a pitiful cry was heard.

How it rang out through the forest! It sounded almost human. What could it be? Alila's father jumped up and crept through the woods in the direction of the sound. His boy followed close at his heels. They had gone but a short distance when a strange sight met their eyes. High up on the branch of a tree lay a huge boa-constrictor. He must have been a hundred years old, he was so large.

His eyes were fastened upon a poor little deer in the coil of his tail, which he had stretched down to trap his prey as it walked along. Ah! the deer's eyes close and the piteous cry stops as he is clasped more and more tightly in the clutch of the boa. And now the serpent raises him from the ground, and swings him against the trunk of the tree; he is thrown with such force he is instantly killed.

But what were Alila and his father doing all this time? They were too late to save the deer, but the boa did not escape. As he was about to descend the tree to feed upon his victim, his wicked eyes saw the hunters for the first time. Out darted his forked tongue in anger, just as two arrows entered his body and ended his life. The rest of the party came up at this moment and helped cut away the skin of the boa. It would be useful for making dagger sheaths.

Now indeed they would have a grand feast, for they could add the flesh of the deer and boa to what they had already obtained.

CHAPTER XIII
CROCODILES

When dinner was over, they began to look around their stopping-place. They found they were close to a deep river. Should they swim across it, or turn homeward?

"You must not try to cross without a boat," said one of the men to Alila's father. "Crocodiles make their home in these waters. It is possible we may not see any from this shore, but at the same time, if you should try to swim to the other side, you might be attacked suddenly, and be unable to escape. I know one poor fellow who lost his life in this very place.

"Still, if you wish for more sport, I will tell you what to do. Let us all watch on the shore here for signs of crocodiles. We are in no hurry. Have your guns and arrows ready to help if one of the creatures should appear. I will dive into the river and attack him with my spear."

It was a daring thing to think of. As every one knew, there is only one place in the animal's body that can be pierced. That is directly under the fore legs. Even bullets will fly off from any other part of the scaly covering as though they had struck against a stone wall.

If the hunter venture to come close to such a monster, and his dagger fail to pierce the vital spot, there is no help for him. The great jaws will close upon him instantly, and he will never be seen again.

But the quiet Tagals seem to love danger, and no one tried to discourage the hunter. They walked quietly along the river's side for two hours, at least; they were about to turn when Alila cried:

"There he is, close to the bamboo thicket on the shore."

As they looked toward the spot, the fearful head and jaws of a crocodile could be seen reaching up out of the water.

Ready! Down dived the hunter, spear in hand. The attack was sudden and successful. The spear reached the one place it could enter, and stuck fast. The diver did not stop a moment longer, but swam back to the shore to his waiting friends. The surface of the river was instantly streaked with blood as the crocodile plunged through the water in his death agony.

The men waited till the great body of the monster became still and quiet. Then with the aid of rattan nooses they drew it up on the shore, and with their sharp knives proceeded to strip away the skin.

"It is a good medicine for rheumatism. I know it will cure the bad pains from which my mother suffers," said Alila's father.

"And I will take some of the flesh and dry it as a cure for asthma," said another of the party. "I know a man who suffers very much from the trouble. He will be glad to be able to breathe easily once more."

It was now near night and too late to think of starting home. They must camp out once more. Every one hoped to be free from the persistent leeches this time. They made a fire and stretched themselves beside it.

CHAPTER XIV
TONDA'S STORY

"Tonda, do tell us some of your adventures," begged Alila. "You have travelled so far and seen such wonderful things! Father says you have even been to the great city of Manila. I wonder what a city can be like."

Tonda had certainly seen more of the world than any one Alila knew, and he was always proud and glad to show his knowledge. So, although he was tired and sleepy from the excitement of the day, he began to tell of his visit to Manila when a young man.

"Oh, a city is indeed a wonderful place, Alila; I believe you would be almost frightened, at first, at the queer noises you would hear.

crowd of people at city gate
"'AROUND ONE PART OF THE CITY THERE IS A STRONG WALL'"
"What would you think of long, heavy cars rushing along through the streets with no buffaloes to draw them and a single pony in their place? These cars run along on tracks through streets in which round stones are set in, side by side.

"There are great buildings divided by walls into many different rooms. Around one part of the city there is a strong wall which was built long, long ago, I was told. Behind those walls the people used to fight against their enemies and were safe.

"There is a river running right through the city, and upon it many kinds of boats sail at every hour of the day and night. While I was there, the Chinese had a grand festival. Great ships like floating palaces rode up and down the river. At night they were lighted up from topmast to stern. Bands of music kept playing, and every morning the Chinese who filled the vessels threw squares of coloured paper over the sides and burned incense in honour of St. Nicholas, in whose memory they held the festival.

"Why was St. Nicholas honoured so? Because in far distant times he saved the life of a Chinaman from the fury of a crocodile.

"It happened in this way. The man was sailing on the river in a small canoe, with no thought of danger. All at once, a crocodile appeared close to the boat, capsized it, and with open jaws was ready to devour the man. It was a fearful moment, but the Chinaman did not lose hope. He lifted up his voice in prayer to St. Nicholas, and begged him to save his life. The good saint appeared before him, and, striking the crocodile with his wand, changed it instantly into a rock.

"The man was saved, but you may be sure he did not forget the wonderful help he had received. He went back to Manila, and with the help of his friends built a chapel in honour of the saint. Every year since then the Chinese have gathered in the city and remembered the day when their countryman's life was saved. They hold one festival after another during two whole weeks. The people say that the city is always a gay sight at such times."

By the time this story was finished, the company gathered around the fire began to nod their heads. They were so tired from the day's hard work that they could listen no longer. A minute afterward Alila was sound asleep. He knew nothing more till the sunlight fell upon him the next morning.

On the way home two more boars and a deer were shot. A bamboo hurdle was quickly made, and the store of flesh was placed on it and easily carried on the shoulders of the men.

CHAPTER XV
STRANGE NEIGHBOURS

You can imagine how glad Alila's mother was to see him back once more, safe and sound. She kissed him tenderly in the odd fashion of her people. When he had told her all his adventures, he said:

"Oh, mother, I want to go again. I haven't seen half of the strange things in those forests. And, besides, hunters have told me of queer people who live high up in the mountains beyond us. They are very wild, and have such strange customs. It is said that they lived in these islands before our people came here, hundreds and hundreds of years ago. They must have been driven up into the thick forests to save themselves from being captured.

"The men call them Negritos. They are very black, and do not look at all like us. Their hair is a great ball of curls. They do not know much more than animals."

"Yes, my child, I have not only heard about these savages, I have seen one of them," replied his mother. "Your father has been among them, and will tell you about their queer ways of living. They have no homes, but sleep at night under the trees. If you heard them talking, you would think at first it was the chattering of monkeys. They have very few words in their language.

"When they plant their gardens, they do not plough them as we do. They only scrape away the top of the earth, and then scatter their seed. They do not even clear places in the forests."

While she was telling Alila these things, his father was not there. As soon as he got back from the hunt, he went off to look over the farm to see if the hemp was growing well. When he returned from this work Alila went up to him, and said:

"Why is it, father, you have never told me about the Negritos? I never even heard of them till I went on the hunt with you and your friends."

"I knew how you like daring deeds, my boy, and felt you would be anxious to go among these savages and see them for yourself. So I waited till you should be older. Now you have shown how much you can bear, I will take you into strange places, and you shall see things for yourself. The Negritos are a cowardly race, yet they are dangerous; they always use poisoned arrows, and, from their safe hiding-places in the mountains, often succeed in killing any people who dare to come near them."

Then he told Alila how the Negrito children are taught to use their bows and arrows when very young. They learn to shoot so well they can hit the fish swimming in the water. They seldom fail to hit what they aim at.

These savages live mostly on roots and fruits. Still, they do know how to make a fire and cook some of their game. But they have no dishes, and the bird or animal to be eaten is thrown among the embers and allowed to stay there till the outside is burned to a crisp. When any one among them is very ill, they do not wait for him to die, but bury him alive.

One of the most laughable things Alila's father ever saw was a Negrito wedding. The young bride pretended to run away from her future husband. After he had caught her, they were carried up a bamboo ladder by their friends, and sprinkled with water out of a cocoanut shell. Then they came down and knelt on the ground, and an old man touched their heads together. That made them man and wife.

Alila was much interested, and begged his father to tell more stories of the Negritos and other savage tribes living in the depths of the island forests.

He listened to tales of the Igorrotes, who live in huts like beehives and creep into them like insects. They are people whom the white men have tried again and again to conquer and to teach of God, but they prefer to go naked and lead their own savage life.

And then his father described to him some of the sights he had seen. He told him of a wonderful cave right there in his own island of Luzon. It was equal in beauty to the cave Aladdin himself had entered.

Wonderful pendants of crystallised lime reached down from the lofty roof, shining like diamonds. There were pillars of the snowy lime a hundred feet in height, glittering in dazzling beauty. There were spacious halls leading one from another in this underground palace. It was a dangerous journey into this wonderful cave, but sometime Alila must go there, his father said.

He should visit the volcano island, too,—an island in the middle of a lake, from which terrible floods of lava and boiling water have poured forth many times. What sorrow and destruction it has caused!

A long, long time ago, the boy's father cannot tell how many years have passed, there was a terrible eruption. It lasted for many days. There were quakings of the earth and horrible sounds under ground. The air was filled with darkness save for flashes of lightning. Great columns of mud and sand arose from out the lake. Torrents of lava poured over the sides of the volcano and destroyed whole villages on the shores of the lake.

Ah! it was a fearful time for the people, and few of those who were there lived to tell the story to their children.

Alila's eyes grew larger as he listened to the wonders of the world around him. Yes, he would travel and see these things for himself. He was growing impatient. He could not wait much longer, for now he was nearly a man grown.

Sometime, let us hope, we shall meet our little Alila. We will ask him what he himself has learned that no one else can tell us.

CHAPTER XVI
THE STOUT-HEARTED SAILOR

Although Alila is anxious to travel and learn more of this great round world, yet his own people seldom leave their island home. Strange to say, however, white travellers from distant lands began to visit these shores hundreds of years ago.

The first one to do this was a brave admiral named Ferdinand Magellan. What wonderful adventures filled the life of this man! It seems almost like a fairy tale.

After Columbus made his famous voyages across the Atlantic and discovered America, Magellan, who lived in Portugal, was much excited over the news. The world must certainly be round, he thought, and he was no longer satisfied to explore the waters near his own home. He, too, wished to find new and distant lands; but this was not enough. He felt sure he could discover a way to the countries of the East, rich in silks, spices, and precious gems, by sailing west.

The King of Portugal was a powerful ruler and anxious for new possessions, yet he did not encourage Magellan. Instead of this, he was ordered to go back to Africa and keep on fighting against the Moors, for he had already won many victories there. The king was even stern to him for leaving the war in Africa. Why had he returned to Portugal to ask for other work than what had been given him?

It was a sad disappointment, and Magellan turned away from the king's presence with a bitter heart. It was almost impossible for him to keep from bursting into tears, though he was a brave, strong man. Just as he was leaving the palace, an old friend stopped him and whispered:

"Why do you not go to the King of Spain and ask his help? He is young, to be sure, but he will be glad to get the services of a brave man from any country, for he is anxious to gain new lands and greater power."

Magellan's first thought was, "I cannot leave the service of my own country for that of another." But afterward he said to himself, "No, I am not right in working for one king when I can do more for the world in serving another. I feel that I shall do much yet. And I am willing to dare great risks, and give my life even, for the sake of what is not yet known."

He went to Spain and offered his services to King Charles. You will be pleased to know that this king was the grandson of the very Isabella who so nobly helped Columbus. The young king was filled with the spirit of his grandmother. He said to Magellan:

"Your plan is good; you are daring, yet cautious; you shall have ships and supplies. So be of good courage and prepare for your voyage."

Magellan's heart bounded with joy. He promised the king that wherever he should land in places not discovered before, there he would plant the flag of Spain. He also vowed that he would do his best to teach the Christian religion to the heathen and that a goodly company of priests should go with him to baptise all who were willing.

At last the great day came when Magellan set sail. Shortly before, he was married to one whom he had long loved and whom, alas! he should never see again after leaving the shores of Spain. He and his fair young wife had watched the building and repairing of the ships which were to sail away with him so soon. With her at his side, he had studied the rude maps of the Atlantic Ocean made by earlier voyagers, and the instruments which should aid him in managing the fleet.

The great moment arrived at last. Amidst the shouts of the people, the peals of the bells, and the roaring of the cannon, the anchors were lifted and the fleet sailed into the West.

Days passed quietly by. The weather was good, and Magellan, now Admiral Magellan, watched constantly for land. Many wonderful things were seen by the sailors as they crossed the broad Atlantic. There were shoals of flying-fish, strange and interesting birds, besides immense sharks that followed the ships for days at a time.

After a voyage of over two months, the coast of South America came in sight. The fleet stopped at different places; at one time finding themselves among friendly savages, at another among a race of unfriendly giants. Each time the ships were headed farther and farther south.

At this time Magellan had other troubles besides directing the fleet. You remember that he was a Portuguese, although he was sailing under the King of Spain. So it happened that while some of the sailors were from Magellan's country, most of them were Spaniards. These latter were jealous of their leader because he belonged to a different nation from themselves. Some of them talked secretly together and made a plan to imprison him and take possession of the ships.

But Magellan learned of their wicked plot in time to defeat them, and he punished them as they deserved. Only a cool and daring man could have succeeded in defeating so many strong enemies. But he did succeed, and the ships sailed onward as though nothing had happened.

It grew colder and colder. A violent storm arose and the ships were tossed about like leaves in the wind. But Magellan was without fear and kept his men filled with courage. At length he reached a narrow passage leading to the west. He said to his captains:

"I believe we have come to the end of this continent. If we can make our way through this strait we shall look upon the new ocean."

And the brave explorer sailed safely through the dangerous strait now named for him. The storm passed away, and one bright, clear morning Magellan looked for the first time upon a new and vast extent of water. It was the dreamed-of ocean. It looked so calm and peaceful that he said, "I will call it 'Pacific,' for I have never seen the like before."

Weeks were spent upon these waters. They were so quiet that for days at a time the ships could not advance. There was hardly a breath of wind.

And now it was discovered that the supplies were getting low. The sailors thought of home so far away, of friends they might never see again; they pictured death by starvation here in the midst of these beautiful waters. The food was served out in smaller and smaller portions to the unhappy men. At last they were told there was nothing left to satisfy their hunger save the rats which infested the ships and some ox-hides which had been used to protect the rigging.

Think for a moment of the condition of Magellan and those with him. They were out of sight of land in the midst of an unknown ocean. Some were already dying of thirst; others were too sick and weak to help in the care of the ship. Do you wonder that the sailors felt bitter at the one who had brought them here and was the cause of their suffering? But Magellan did not give up courage, even now. He ordered the hides to be softened in the sea water and then boiled. For some days longer the crews managed to live on with this for food.

One morning, when hope was nearly gone, a fresh breeze from the east filled the sails of the ships, and in a few hours Magellan saw land in the distance. The men's hearts beat hard for joy at the welcome sight. They soon reached a small island where ripe fruits were abundant, and where they could provide fresh supplies for the ships.

But they did not stay many days, for Magellan was not even now ready to give up his search for the famous lands of the East. He felt that, as the world was round, he must surely be near them by this time. So once more the ships set sail, and soon reached the shores of one of the Philippines, but a short distance from Alila's home. It looked so rich and beautiful that the ships anchored once more, and the admiral ordered the sick men to be taken on shore. Large tents were set up, and the sufferers were nursed back to health and strength. There was an abundance of good pure water and fresh food. All were soon well and strong.

There were no people living on this island, but two days after he arrived Magellan saw some canoes out upon the water. They were coming swiftly toward the camp. They were filled with natives of another island near by, who had seen the ships of the strangers; they were curious to look upon the white men who were living near them.

These people of Alila's race had soft yellow skins and beautiful white teeth. They wore no clothing except aprons made of bark. They danced around the great admiral as he stood on the shore dressed in his most elegant garments, and laughed and shouted. They wished him to see they were friendly. They offered fresh fish and palm wine, cocoanuts and figs, while Magellan made them wildly happy by giving them looking-glasses and bells, ivory toys and brass trinkets. As he found them honest and peaceful, he allowed them to go on board his ships. He ordered his men to fire the cannon to amuse them, but the noise frightened them so much that some of them jumped into the water and came near drowning.

The chief of these people came to see the Spaniards. His face was painted, and he wore heavy gold earrings and bracelets. He was kind and pleasant. He brought a boat-load of fruit and, best of all, some chickens.

Magellan learned from these people that he was near still richer and larger islands. After a few days he started out once more. He passed island after island, sometimes landing on their shores, sometimes sailing slowly along, drawing a map of these new and wonderful places.

At the island of Cebu, Magellan made friends with the king, who was baptised by the priests, and pretended to become a Christian. A large cross bearing a wooden crown was set up on the top of a high hill near the shore. It was a token to all travellers who should come this way that this land now belonged to the King of Spain.

While the white visitors were staying here, the King of Cebu did all he could to entertain them. He seemed anxious to show how friendly he felt toward them. The Spanish sailors were much interested in the strange customs and festivals of the brown people. They noticed that the food was only half cooked and then heavily salted. This made the eaters very thirsty, and quite ready to drink quantities of palm wine afterward. They sucked this through long reeds of bamboo. They were always glad to have the sailors share their feasts and entertainments.

Just as the fleet was about to set sail again, something happened to change Magellan's plans. The King of Cebu was in trouble. The people of another island over whom he was also the ruler were coming to make war upon him. Could the brave admiral refuse help, when the king had treated him so kindly? Surely not. He said to the king:

"Let me go against these rebels and make peace for you. I have cannons which I will use, and other weapons of war such as they have never seen before. They will be easily terrified, and quickly submit to your rule."

So it was that Magellan and sixty of his followers sailed against the enemy. But when they arrived at the island they found a large army ready to meet them. The warriors carried sharp spears, bows, and poisoned arrows, and each man was protected by a wooden shield. They stood upon the side of a hill. As Magellan and his men landed and advanced toward them, they rushed down upon the Spaniards with fury, surrounding them on all sides.

The great leader was calm and brave as usual, but there was little hope for success. In another hour he had fallen, a noble victim to his savage foes. Many of his followers fell by his side; the rest managed to escape to the ships and sail back to Cebu to tell the sad news to the king.

Thus ended the life of the noble Magellan, the first white man to cross the broad waters of the Pacific, the first one to show others it was indeed possible to sail around the world.

He was unlike many who lived in those old days,—for he did not care for gold or great possessions. He only wished to know more of this wonderful world, and to help others to greater wisdom. He gave his life for one whom he thought had need of help.

How did the King of Cebu act when he learned of the leader's death? He turned against those of his followers who were left, and they were obliged to depart in haste.

They made still other discoveries of great value. At length, sailing around the continent of Africa, they returned to Spain to tell of the brave deeds of their dead leader, the great admiral and navigator, and their own strange adventures.

They were the first men to sail around the world.

THE END